Joan Smokes

Angela Meyer

CONTRABAND

Published by Contraband,
an imprint of Saraband,
Digital World Centre,
1 Lowry Plaza,
The Quays, Salford, M50 3UB
www.saraband.net

ISBN: 9781912235742

1 3 5 7 9 8 6 4 2

Printed and bound in Great Britain by
Clays Ltd, Elcograf S.p.A.

MIX
Paper from
responsible sources
FSC® C018072
FSC
www.fsc.org

*This is the winning novella
in the inaugural (2019)
Mslexia Novella Award.*

The fascination of what's difficult
Has dried the sap out of my veins, and rent
Spontaneous joy and natural content
Out of my heart.

—from 'The Fascination of What's Difficult',
W.B. YEATS

VAST, EMPTY RED CRAGS. There are bombs in the desert, she'd read. She is moving toward the light. Need to be blasted, need heat, to bare skin to scorching. Need to radiate the piled-on pain of thirty-three years. Need the heat in order to need less, to melt herself down. Fingers on the wheel. Bare basics – money, food, sleep, touch.

The last time they made love, he must have known. As she'd leaned over to put on her creams and take her pill and turn off the lamp, he had trailed his fingers down her spine, traced them from hip to hip and up along her curved side. She felt his eyes on her skin, a rare thing in itself. She had taken her time over the creams, the pill, reaching toward the lamp. Holding this touch, faint with it.

Blink. Don't think about it.

SHE'D SEEN THE LAS Vegas strip in a movie. It is just as technicolour in real life. The radio plays 'Be My Baby' by the Ronettes and she flicks it off because love songs are ice. The lights make sound in her eyes. On one sign: the soprano crescendo of pink. On another, a swooshing fan of green-blue. Everything is tall. The buildings, the cars, waterfalls and feathers. It is orange desert dusk. She does not know where to go. The money has to stretch out until she gets a job. So where is the off-strip, less tall area where the workers live? But she *could* just pull in here, under this sparkling roof, and let the valet park the car. She could walk into that casino and play the games her father used to play in Brisbane. Swear like him. Drink like him. Another dead man. *Don't think about it*. She's not dressed for the casino, she supposes. She will find a place to sleep and come out in the day and take care of that. She should probably swap out this old Anglia anyway, just in case anyone wants to find her. She feels confident she can disappear, here, change her name. Become tall.

Send a letter to Mother:

Jack is dead. I am staying in America.

No, lie.

Past the strip and there's a more squat neon sign, buzzing pink: vacancy vacancy vacancy. Pull up in front of the reception. Smooth down the hair around her part. Press lips together to spread any remaining lipstick. Push the door open and it jangles. Smile.

ON A NOTEPAD IN her handbag is a list:

    Beth Spencer

    Rose Mulvane

    Liv Smythe

    Jane Hancock

    Helen Bastion

    Sylvia Barry

    Joan West

JOAN SMOKES. SHE BUYS a packet of cigarettes from the machine in the concrete corridor. Her room is three doors down. She opens the door. An apple-skin tang over something more stale. She will get her suitcase soon. First, she unbuttons her dress and steps out of it – it is hot – and turns the dial on the television. She wriggles up onto the head of the bed in her cream bra, panties, suspenders and stockings, and settles into the pillows. She opens the packet of cigarettes and puts one in her mouth. She has no lighter. She sighs. She holds it there, thinking about the way Jack would hold a cigarette in his mouth. She had shared them with him sometimes, when they'd been drinking and close. She takes the cigarette out of her mouth and sits it in the ashtray on the little fake-marble bedside table. There is a rim of pink on it now, from her lipstick. She puts both hands over her belly, as she has that sensation coming – that inward, sucking black hole, as though she were about to implode. The emptiness makes her gasp. Watch the TV. Bette Davis. Look at the things other women bear on their faces.

ONE MAN IS AS good as another, her mother said.

You can let the feelings develop.

Her mother was frustrated. Her girl had turned down Reggie and Ben already. You're getting fussy, her mother said. But there was something she knew inside herself – a certain capacity that wasn't being filled. And then Jack came along and it was filled, in moments. But filled entirely, in those moments, so there was no going back, no matter what happened around those moments, no matter the moments he lived entirely in his own head. They met at a dance in Brisbane, during the war – American soldiers, Australian women. Or, mainly, girls. Gloves and tulle, sweat. She observed her friend's lip trembling and thought about the parts of a woman they kept to themselves, looking at the men like pieces of caramel, dancing with them and inhaling whatever was at head height, enjoying the men's noses in their hair. There was a war on. And the men were in some small position of control over the outcome, or were connected to that control, and that made them powerful – their uniforms; their fit, straight bodies.

Jack's eyes were a startling pale blue. He smiled confidently, as though he saw her secret parts. Only later would she come to know what it took for him to develop that way of seeming sure about things, and how it was already what she could sense beneath that, what many women could – the vulnerability – that made his eyes seem bluer. Because rarely did you get to look into them.

He was beautiful, a beautiful man. But that's a kind of power a man can find uncomfortable.

JOAN WAKES IN THE motel room and watches the dust motes float across the air. Light is streaming in through the thin blind. Today is a day of tasks. She doesn't want to get up. But stay here too long and the thoughts will curdle.

Swap the car. Buy a lighter. Find a job.

She gets up and thinks about what dress most befits Joan. Something floral, something fitting. She will wear the red lipstick, curl her hair.

Add to list:

Dye hair. Dark. Joan has dark hair, like Liz Taylor.

Like Jack.

Yes, well.

The lighter first. Joan would have a cigarette with her coffee. Black, strong coffee.

Once she is dressed she drives to a diner down the road, down the off-strip. She sits in a red booth and orders a black coffee. Black for the empty stomach. They sell her a cheap lighter and she holds the flame to her sober cigarette. Inhaling sends swirls to her head, and she leans back into the leather. She supposes she should eat something.

There is a little boy staring at her from the booth across. Children always stare. She smiles at him and he turns away. She sits back up taller, getting used to the cigarette. She refuses to feel sad every time she sees a child, but something happens to her physically. Ache is too soft a word.

She orders some bacon and toast. She will just eat a bit of it.

Everything is bright and glinting. This butter, the clean table, the child's hair.

THE CAR SALESMAN IS condescending, in that way men are. But Joan knows how to deal with it. She is older than she looks and will have none of it. She doesn't want something so big anymore, she tells him. And refuses the first three bombs he shows her. Even she, as a woman, can see they are all rust. In the fourth one, the driver's seat and steering wheel feel right. The view out over the hood feels right. It is more expensive but what else is she going to use the money for?

And she will get a job. She will definitely find a job.

This kind of trust is not something she had in the old life. But when Jack was gone she untwisted. There is no more wondering about what he thinks and feels, what he wants, how they affect each other. There is no worrying left.

IN THE HAIR PARLOUR the young woman asks questions, and Joan has to find her voice, and tell the woman that she just arrived, that she is looking for a job.

'What brings you to Vegas?'

'I'd rather not talk about it.'

'Oh, that's perfectly alright. There are a lot of folks here for all kinds of reasons. Me, I grew up in Nevada. I probably won't ever leave. Are you English or something?'

'Australian, but I've been in America for a while.'

'Well, this colour is going to suit your complexion just fine. You'll see.'

The young woman's reassuring tone, and the way she looks into Joan's eyes in the mirror, and those fingertips gentle at her neck. Why is it that women can so readily care for strangers?

'Thank you,' says Joan. Manages a smile.

When the dryer is on it blasts out all noise, which is calming, and she looks out at her new powder blue car. There is a small, unfamiliar tickle of excitement in her belly. Colour and heat to start all over.

JOAN PUSHES COINS INTO the slot and each *pling* satisfies her ears, and the *cjunk cjunk* grind of the handle as she pulls it down, and then *sluck sluck* as each row comes into place, revealing cherries and mustard cans and cowboy hats, never completely lined up, but she won't play for too long; she just wanted to see the inside of a casino. There aren't many women alone, except working. In the bar, walking around in slippery dresses with trays full of champagne cocktails and old fashioneds, or coins, and she also saw a troupe of showgirls in olive green feather-tails.

Greens. The first many times she saw him he was always in green, in uniform. She remembers that first time she saw the other him, after an Australian soldier made a crack about his hat. They sat by the river afterwards and he was quiet and fuming.

'Do you think it's too big across here?' he asked her, pulling his uniform out at the sides of his chest.

'No, I think it fits just fine.'

'You're just saying that to make me feel better.'

His eyes were cold and closed-off; his skin

almost looked paler, sheened with sweat. She took his hand, to reassure him.

'Those fuckers don't understand what we're doing for them, this country.'

She flinched at the swear word, but said, 'They're just intimidated. It's bravado.'

He frowned.

Then it was like the sun came back up.

'Yeah,' he said, 'You're right.'

And he squeezed her hand and smiled and seemed to shake the thoughts out of his head.

'Sorry. Sometimes I get really... furious.'

'That's okay,' she said.

That's okay. It's okay. It'll be okay. I'm here. They're not out to get you. No one is out to get you. I love you. You're safe. It'll be okay.

If she had known that he never would have believed her, or not for long at a time, what would she have done?

Eighteen years.

Sluck sluck sluck – so close to three cherries, and she draws on her cigarette and waits for the girl to bring her a champagne cocktail.

'Love,' she says, as that's what Joan calls other women, 'How does one get a job around here?'

THEY STILL COME AT four a.m., the thoughts about Sylvia – the young redhead who'd lived next door to them. Thoughts about how perfectly round her arse looked in those gingham shorts, how he must have been noticing it too. How a man so sensual must notice other women like that, and think about them.

When the door to his room was closed – she thought of it as his room, not the spare room – and it was quiet in there. And she strained to hear but didn't want to, and sometimes even blocked her ears with her hands to stop herself from straining. When he wasn't playing his guitar, was he just lying there in his own head? Was he thinking about her? No. Was he thinking about Sylvia, or another woman? Was he touching himself? How often did he touch himself? Such a sensual man must touch his own body. Such a sexual man must take his own pleasure. Especially when, for a whole weekend, he would be apart from her, in that room of his own.

Why, now, does she still think of Sylvia and experience that rush of fury and fear? Because she still cannot ever really know. How does the mind learn to let things go? She twists in the scratchy sheets. It is too light in this room, neon flare. She needs to add to her list: eye mask. What does Joan do with four a.m. thoughts? She reaches for the packet of cigarettes, and the remote. If there is no one here to curl towards, to take comfort with, she needs banal voices, dull cut-outs of people, well-dressed neat people coming in and out of frame.

IN THE BRIGHT CASINO, in the day-night nowhere, the four a.m. thoughts are settled somewhere at the base of the spine, and not a bother. Daytime is being together and capable. She is upright and strong and sexy in her uniform. She practices her exercises on the floor of her room. The chest and back are taught, the belly dips in at the button, the ankle is elegant after the curve of the calf muscle, leading into red, glittering pumps.

She is attending the floor with May, a redhead with dimples and big teeth. Young but motherly. Showing Joan the ropes. Joan is still getting used to the tray, not tilting or tipping it and spilling the cocktails. The good thing is that no one asks her any questions. They're all in their flashing-light worlds. They take a moment over the drink to eyeball her figure, then they get back to feeding the slots. She witnesses her first jackpot. A machine makes fireworks and trumpets and her floor manager rushes down into the pit. The winner has his arms lifted as though someone were holding a gun to him. Big rings of blue sweat. Eyebrows to the sky, but silent. Completely speechless. Everyone around him doubles down, feeds harder, faces pinched, backs curved over like shamed dogs.

On her way out of the casino, aching from hips to toes, she hears the doorman say, 'Goodnight Miss West.' Halfway across the car park she remembers that 'Miss West' is her. She turns back and he is still looking after her, a young black man. She smiles awkwardly in apology and sends half a wave.

HE WENT TO THE cinema for the newsreels. He read everything coming out about what had happened. He told her all about the Nuremberg trials while she was at the sink, his face haunted and emphatic. All about the gas chambers. About the purses made from humans.

'I don't want to know,' she said.

'But everyone should know,' he said.

He wanted to think about the faces of people while they were being tortured. She saw the whirring in him, the wanting to understand. So it won't happen to him? Or so he would never do it to someone else? His eyes were so wide and she thought of him as broken when he was like this. Like a stuck clock. She'd touch him gently, wanting to soothe, but he'd flinch. Madder at her than at the Nazis. Mad at her vulnerability and softness. She never knew what to do. He was so difficult. But you cannot tell a difficult person they are difficult, because the difficulty then turns towards you – that self-protectiveness.

'I am not your enemy,' she wanted to tell him, but instead she asked if he would like a cup of tea.

THERE IS A RICH, composed woman at this table, with tight curls. There's a short man with his cowboy hat tipped back. And a big man with a dark moustache. She's seen him before. He keeps winning and begins to think Joan is good luck. He presses the sweaty die into her palm. She smiles at him, for the tip.

His suit is a thick material, rich black, a little silken under the lights. His attention is relieving. He isn't her type – wouldn't look good in swim shorts – but he has a confident smell about the cheeks and hair, making her want to lean in close.

She walks across the floor to refresh her tray, pausing when she sees two policemen standing in the yellow light of a chandelier. The gamblers are giving them a wide berth. Something goes cold in her stomach. She goes to the furthest side of the bar, away from them. They are looking for someone. Who are they looking for?

Her hands shake a little when she picks up the tray of cocktails. She has to concentrate on the step and wiggle. She glances at them, and is relieved to see them now talking with the casino manager, actually smiling, as he shepherds them toward a door in the wall.

She feels foolish. That was an old life, and all questioning had been tied off.

Just these last couple of steps to the table but she's gone jelly-like and when the big gambler reaches for a drink she somehow misses putting her foot down correctly and the cocktails topple forward in the tray. Her arms reach around to catch the glasses but that means the liquid and bits of fruit spray out the sides and all over her, too. She stands still, looking down, not sure how to recover. The lights and the laughter and the sounds of the slots, the whir of the wheels, the tuk of the dice – all goes on. A firm hand is at her elbow and she is being steered back down the stairs. He whispers in her ear, 'Don't worry sweetheart, it'll all be forgotten in about twenty minutes.'

It is the big gambling man. His face is gentle and open. When the bar manager sees her coming the anger in his eyes is only a flicker, and he smiles warmly at her escort.

'It was my fault,' says the gambler. 'Give her the night off.'

'Of course.'

The gambler turns to Joan. 'You have something other than your uniform, sweetheart?'

'Yes.'

'Come join me when you're cleaned up.'

There is no question in it.

THE HOUSE WAS LIKE a cardboard box. Little cement ramp up to the front door, patchy grass and a few rose bushes in the front yard. One huge oak out the back, bringing character, but threatening to crush them in every storm. The first time she got pregnant she asked Jack to at least saw off some of the branches. He didn't and she called an arborist, and when she put her hands across her tummy the man did them a good deal. She hadn't told Jack yet about the pregnancy. The house was cardboard and Jack knew it but he had simply bought the first house he'd come across that they could afford. She did her best, finding a teal settee to match the cornices, buying matching lavender towels from the discount department store. Everything became pilled and stiff, and the house was hot in summer and cold in winter, but there were times, waking up with him in the cold, and he wrapped his arms around her from behind and held so tight, squeezing the sad hours from her. In those moments she knew he was trying to remember to be there. Sometimes he would fuck her, from behind like that, and sometimes he would get up and throw on the clothes she'd

22

sat on the chair and make a coffee and head out the door to work. Sometimes he would kiss her goodbye and sometimes not. Either way she found it hard to find her legs and get up after he left. The smell of him and the reminder of closeness and warmth in the bed. The empty cardboard lounge room and kitchen waiting. Bits of grit caught in the carpet.

OUTSIDE THE CASINO IS a dark blue limousine; the lights glint off its curved and polished surface. The gambler's driver, a black man in a neat tux, opens the back doors for them on each side in turn. Joan settles on the leather and opens her purse for a cigarette. The gambler reaches for a bottle of champagne – opened – and pours her a glass.

'I'm more of a gin girl,' she says, but takes it anyway.

The car starts moving. The windows are almost too dark to see out. The gambler is staring at her in this small and close space.

'May I open a window?'

'It's cold.'

She puts her cigarette in her drink hand and winds down the window anyway. The pink dusk flattens the effect of the neon signs.

'It's a beautiful night,' she says.

'It is now,' he says.

She looks at him properly, gives a wry smile.

'You have a hint of an accent,' he says.

'Australian.'

'Did you come to Vegas to become a showgirl?'

'Yes,' she says, going with it. 'What is your name?'

'Oliver.'

'The Oliver in my gin.'

He smiles. 'Could you close that window?' He is dressed much more warmly than her.

'I guess you've seen it a thousand times.'

'I guess I have.'

She has finished her cigarette and he reaches for her spare hand. His is warm and encompasses hers. She thinks she should feel afraid but she doesn't.

His suite is a mansion. He encourages her to take off her heels and her feet sink into, are massaged, by the carpet. He has three types of gin in the bar and Joan points at one, decides this is her favourite. And actually she has her martini with a twist, thank you.

The view is of a darkened desert, and he tells her he can see the nuclear tests from here.

'We should go out some time; it's quite the spectacle. And their days are numbered. We'll take a picnic.'

She nods, walks around the room. There are lamps, side tables, ashtrays, gold suns in the décor, and no pictures. One lampshade ascends from a bronze lion. The lounge is pure white, the bedding too. She is so pale that if she were naked, she could disappear in it. The way he looks at her, he is waiting for this moment. She should see what it is like. Resisting could make it worse. She sits on the end of the bed, places down her glass. He walks to the wardrobe and removes his jacket. In the wardrobe, she can see dresses, skirts, blouses. It is too late to back out.

SHE ENTERED THE CARDBOARD door with two paper bags in her arms and said hello to the back of his head, glued to *The Twilight Zone*. He said 'hi' darkly and didn't look at her or get up to help, and her heart rate went up, knowing immediately he was in *that place* – from his voice, his body language, the almost visible barrier around him. In the kitchen, she set down the bags and began to unpack them. On the bench she saw an opened envelope and piece of paper. She scanned it: a cheerful letter from his mother. It made her fearful, made her need to go to the toilet. She wished he would tell her more about why he was always affected like this when he heard from his mother, or his older sister. To ask him directly was to risk being shut out for days.

She pulled two beers out of the fridge and went in to the lounge room. The curtains were drawn and the room was heavy with smoke. She handed him a beer and he took it without thanks. She set hers down and sat on the lounge's arm, closest to him, and ran a hand through his thinning hair. His eyes crinkled at her – part annoyance, part gratitude. It was a child-like look. He didn't move away. He put a hand on her leg, kept watching this show he loved. Anything that frightened him, he loved.

'I saw old man Fredricks watering his garden today,' he said flatly.

'Mmm?'

He scoffed. 'I was just looking at him, out there after the rain, drowning his garden, and I thought he was such a cunt.'

Her heart raced by his ear, but she hoped he couldn't hear it. The vitriol in his voice, the strange edge of paranoia.

'Okay.'

'I was just thinking about how foolish people are.' He was almost hissing with rage.

'Sometimes, yes.'

He could sense her not entirely wanting to go along with it, and he stopped, sipped at his beer.

'Anyway.'

She didn't ask about the letter. She didn't ask about the latest with his boss, someone he also became furious about. Though, when he was recalling an incident at work, she hated that often she could see the boss's side. Knowing what it would be like to work with him. She was clenching her teeth. The room was too dark. She simultaneously wanted to go out the back, into the warm evening, and curl up here with his head on her lap, try to massage away the bad, bad thoughts. She stayed where she was, doing neither.

FROM THE BACK OF the car Joan sees the land-scape flatten out, all orangey with tufts of grass. A vastness and calm. They pull up next to other cars in the dust and the driver opens her door. She and Oliver walk, crunch underfoot, to a wooden bleacher where spectators are already gathered – some in casual clothing, some in military fatigue. Oliver told her to dress comfortably, so she has on a collared blouse and pants, low-heeled wedges. He climbs up first and puts out his hand for her. Then he sits the small pillow that's been tucked under his other arm on the wooden seat for her. She's not used to such gestures and they move her too much, create a catch in the throat. She has to pretend this is normal for Joan. She can't tell yet whether Oliver is kind or whether these are just behaviours. You teach a puppy to sit, stay, beg, and reward it; you teach another puppy nothing, just leave it outside in all weather with a bowl. Is one fundamentally a 'better' dog than the other?

'It's a full operation they're testing today,' Oliver explains, and points out the jeeps, the trenches, the troop formations.

They're told it is time to put on the dark glasses they have been handed, or else turn away from the blast.

Joan puts on her dark glasses and sees the desert as blueish. Everything goes quiet. The spectators lean forward. The machine that looks like a catapult makes a cracking sound and the bomb flies off, arcing with a ribbon of smoke toward its destination. The desert lights up when it lands, like a powerful lightning strike, light like an orgasm, Joan thinks, and at first there is white silence. And then a cloud billows from the ground, a thick-looking smoke, and the crack of the blast reaches their ears. Soldiers pop their heads up from trenches and are hit with an almighty sheet of wind, which then reaches the spectators in the stands. It thumps Joan in the chest, like a body pressing down on her. People laugh at the shock of it. Hats have flown off behind the stand. Oliver squeezes her hand and they look at each other, wildly grinning. The soldiers now leap from the trenches and move toward where the cloud is expanding and slowly lifting from the ground – leaping, twisting, like something alive. A helicopter starts up some-where to the west. The stand shakes, as in an earthquake.

Joan is high, excited. She has been blanched, to skull and bones. After eighteen years of small-ness, a cardboard house, a corner of someone's heart and mind, this hot nuclear wind gone through her.

SHE'D KEPT THE FIRST pregnancy from him, not realising beforehand she was able to keep such secrets. And then when it was no longer a pregnancy, there didn't seem any point in telling him. It had been and it was gone, and the oak had shed its branches, and she could deal with the emotions of it the way she'd dealt with everything else.

With the second pregnancy, the information just came out. He was in a light enough mood one evening, cooking dinner for them both and being very proud of himself for doing so: sausages and mash, with caramelised onions. She sat at the dining table making chit chat with him, thinking how beautiful he was, thinking maybe it would change him, that he would be a good dad and show affection like this, like this mood, but all the time.

'I'm pregnant,' she said.

He froze with the masher in his hand. He looked at her, open bright blue eyes.

'We're going to have a baby?'

'Yes,' she smiled. Thinking: well, perhaps.

'Come here,' he said. He held her tightly. She

kissed his neck tenderly, flooded with love. He looked into her eyes. He did everything she'd hoped.

Halfway through dinner, he began to hunch. He chewed each mouthful more slowly. He frowned, sighed, and then stopped eating, lit a cigarette. 'It's too gristly,' he said. 'Disgusting.'

'I think it tastes good,' she said brightly.

'I can't even cook a decent meal,' he said.

She put her own knife and fork down.

'Hey,' she said. 'Look at me.'

'I don't like it when you force me to do that.'

'Sorry,' she said, desperate. *Look up, just look up and let me know you are still here.*

He got up from the table and got a beer out of the fridge. 'I'm gonna watch some TV.'

She sighed.

'What?' he said sharply.

'I thought we were having a nice night.'

'We are,' he said. 'You expect so much.'

He fell asleep on the couch, black and white flicker over his face.

THE DOORMAN WHO ALWAYS greets her is leaving just as she is.

'Hey, Miss West, I'll walk you to your car.'

'Thank you,' she says. Out of uniform he's in a striped polo and tan chinos. Now this man would look good in swim shorts, she thinks – long, lean, broad. They walk to the far corner of the car park, the staff cars.

'How long have you been at The Sands?'

'About a year. They weren't employing us much before that, you know?'

She knew he was referring to the colour of his skin. 'Yes, I had heard that.'

'You haven't been here long either?'

'No.'

'You English or somethin'?'

'Australian.'

He whistles. 'Wow, I know nothing about that.'

'It's far away.'

'I'll say.'

'What are you doing here?'

'It's just where I ended up,' she says.

They reach Joan's car. She leans against it. 'I

saw a bomb go off today,' she smiles.

'Yeah I've seen that.'

'No, I mean I was right there, at the site.'

He frowns. 'You gotta be careful around things like that.'

'It was thrilling, you know.' She leans against the car with one foot on the curb and one hip tilted up and her hands behind herself, all open.

He tilts his head at her. 'Oh yeah?'

'Very.'

He looks side to side, self-consciously. 'Is he a gangster?'

'Who?'

'That man you go around with.'

'I don't think so.'

'I'm not too sure about that.'

People go by. People look at him, her, the stance, the invitation between them. Black white younger older. She opens the driver door and gives him a little nod.

'I know your type.' He smiles, hesitates, then walks around to the passenger door and gets in.

He may, she thinks. He may know better than I do what Joan would do.

'I'm just off strip,' Joan says. 'What do you like to drink?'

'Anything, baby.'

'I have gin.'

'Perfect.' He lights a cigarettes as she is starting up the car, rolls the window right down.

HARVEY THOMAS TALKS DURING the sex: whispers and moans. So here, this is different again. Not the fit and soul-movement of Jack, nor Oliver's snuffling at her parts and a quick pulsing finish, but a clutching and coaxing kind of sex. His young hands are broad across her waist, and that is a kind of containment her body responds to. Like Jack he does not really look much at her face. But she can stare openly at every part of him, smell him subtly, taste him openly. A small nip at the shoulder making him moan. His dark nipples are beautiful on a strong, taut chest.

Afterwards, he gets up and pours himself a drink of water in the bathroom, and she can hear him gulping thirstily. He does not pour her one and she thinks, *Ah, this is more what I am used to.* He will go now, being satiated. He comes back and sits on the bed, staring ahead.

'I can put the TV on,' she says. Jack always wanted to fall asleep to television; it lessened the chance of him having nightmares.

'No, that's alright. Oh, hey, are you thirsty?' He leaps back up. 'I'm sorry, I'm trying to learn not to be selfish.'

'Oh. Yes, please,' she says.

When he brings it back to her she takes it and, still naked, he looks into her eyes and says, 'I didn't always have a lotta love as a kid.' Then he reclines, hands behind his head.

She puts the glass straight down. She is shaking so much she can't bring it to her mouth. He lies there with the open whorl of his ear, dark eyelashes now closed, relaxed. Is it rage or sadness she feels? Some part of her wants to fold him up, squash him down. Her hands shake with the physicality of the compulsion. He is too at ease with such a confession.

She pulls on her slip and sits on the edge of the bed.

'What's wrong, baby?'

'I just want to watch some TV now.'

'Oh… sure.' He stands up and finds his clothes. Joan hears the rustle, the swish, the pulling of laces. He comes over and kisses her on the head. 'I'll see you round.'

'Yes,' she says, not looking at him. 'You will.'

He leaves and she puts the TV on, lights a cigarette. She is not going to cry. But just how easy it had been for him to say that, to her, to a stranger.

Eighteen years.

She had been right, all along. She had known that some people must understand why they were the way they were, notice when their behaviour slipped from normal.

It wasn't really that Jack never completely realised. But he couldn't really put it into words. What had happened to him, what had haunted him, must have been something far worse than she could contemplate, she knew that.

But if he'd been able to find the words.

Just so easily. Harvey had done that so easily. She is shaking so much. She isn't going to cry. She turns the TV up so the blur of voices might take over her. Lying down, she can smell him on the pillow.

SHE CAME HOME FROM the drugstore and walked up the concrete path and past a wilted, brown-tinged rose, into the cardboard house and, immediately – the sound of a woman's voice. She'd been nauseous all morning already from the baby but her legs went hollow now, too. In the lounge room, across from each other, were her husband and the neighbour, the bright woman she often saw hosing in the gingham shorts.

'Hi there,' she said to the woman.

'Oh, I was hoping I'd catch you too,' said the woman, standing and holding out her hand. 'We've waved but haven't had a proper word. I'm Faith.'

'Faith just dropped in to see if we had some butter. Her husband Rodney has the car,' said Jack in his social, performative tone.

'Oh, well, yes, we have plenty,' she said.

'Yes, I got her some,' said Jack, 'and made us tea,' he added proudly.

'Oh, very good,' she said, an absurd rage pulsing in her temple. *So helpful. So friendly to this woman. Falling over himself.*

'Jack was telling me all about Australia in the

war,' Faith said. *So forthcoming.* 'And the way he taught himself poetry. What a clever man.' She looked at her with polite admiration, or congratulation.

At the beginning, Jack had told her about that, too. The sonnets and poems he memorised before the war that would then keep him company on a dark night on a bunk. How he could recite them head to tail. And sometimes, early on, she would lie with him, open and calm, as he recited Yeats: 'I would be – for no knowledge is worth a straw – / Ignorant and wanton as the dawn.' And rarely, now, did he express himself in this way.

'O sweet everlasting Voices...' he began now, and as the woman sat rapt, she thought him a tweeting baby bird for a worm. At first, she had thought the poetry made him deep, complex, but perhaps it was simply a tool that had worked, a way he had shunned rejection, and so with each new person he brought it out, to show his capability.

Mean thoughts, she knew. But that was a reaction to the woman not really knowing him, not seeing it all. And a reaction to so many years with this man, not getting much beyond a poem about something ancient, and distant.

But his genes, now, in her belly. And a consistent, desperate love for him. '...hearts are old...'

Faith left and she tried to stay airy. He postured for a bit about having impressed the neighbour. Here was *his* meanness. She could tell he was saying to her: *I could have her if I wanted. She could want me like you do.*

If she acted wounded, in fact, he would be first meaner and then softer to her. This time she would not. She would ignore him.

'I forgot something,' she said, and grabbed her purse. She felt like she was wrenching her soul from her body. All she wanted was to go to him. But space was most effective at drawing him back in.

THE MOVES WERE CLOSE enough to the exercises she'd been performing for years, alone, on the floor, to keep her shape. She had learned her exercises from a magazine and built upon them over the years when they got too easy. Now, she was being challenged anew. Not just new moves, but surrounded by other, younger, women. And to come: heavy outfits, and an audience. Thankfully, despite Oliver's pushiness, she had only a small role – at the back and mostly in darkness. She enjoyed the training more than practicing the routine – these leg lifts on the floor, tummy-tighteners, twists, balances. She liked how serious and quiet the women were when they were learning. Afterwards they would melt off in giggling, impenetrable huddles. Joan showed she didn't mind. Joan was a shell and of course they saw nothing to gain from befriending her.

Learning the moves gave her a goal, a direction, and Joan was grateful to Oliver for that.

In Oliver's apartment one evening she opened the closet and asked about the women's clothing.

He grit his teeth. 'That's not your concern, sweetheart.'

'Is she still around?' Joan asked, as casually as possible.

'No, and she never will be. That's all you gotta know about it.'

She glanced at the florals, the pastels, the olive green. A woman about her size. Dust had settled lightly on the shoes in the bottom.

'I had a husband,' she said.

She looked at Oliver for his reaction. He sat calmly on the bed, hands in his lap.

'Life's not kind,' he said.

She remembered she was Joan and she closed the closet and went straight over to the bar. 'I'm just making it up as I go along,' she said, pouring gin over ice, adding a dash of soda and a wedge of lemon.

If she died now, what would she leave behind? Cigarette butts in an ashtray, nice lingerie, exercise bands, a wedge of lemon, several unfinished letters to home.

When she lies back down beside Oliver, sees the breath going through his large body, she feels a new tenderness towards him. She is merely a replacement, a comfort, and as long as she knows that, she can play her role. They may now have a new understanding of each other. She had always looked at other couples who didn't have the tension and ache of her and Jack, couples who were so at ease with each other, and she never quite understood the dynamic. She had wondered if easy was real, and better. Was there passion without pain? She is beginning to understand. But Jack had been hers and no one else will ever have that.

SOMETIMES SHE STILL WAKES thinking she hears
a child's footsteps pelting down a carpet hallway.

IT HADN'T REALLY BEEN him, who'd been the violent one. His knuckle joints would turn white with tension but it was her who would throw the pillow, the glass. They would both scream. She would scream and cry in frustration, he in defence, and then she would threaten to walk out, because she needed more, but he would say he wouldn't care – just go – and she couldn't hold the anger, though his callousness hurt worse; she would just crawl into bed with him, and he would be asleep somehow, after all that he would be asleep, and she would wrap around him and he would let her, and would put his hand over hers and give a small squeeze. And she'd be so grateful for the small squeeze that her body would flood with relief – enough to sustain her for days, years.

SHE TRIES ON ONE of the costumes for the first
time. Now that they have practised the routine
again and again, unencumbered, they have to
practice it with the costumes on, to get used
to the weight, the different distribution of balance. This main one has zircons and sapphires,
is a bikini and open skirt, with threads across the
belly and down onto the arms – all for shimmer
in movement. And the headdress sits on as a
cap with a large cockatoo-like fan running front
to back. The green and shimmery white run
through the whole outfit. The women wear sheer
stockings and chunky heels, have large dangling
earrings. Their faces are adorned with powder,
lipstick and false lashes. Joan had dreaded putting on the costume, was worried about being
weighed down, but once it is on, she is looking
in the bright, full-length backstage mirror at a
glamorous but somehow comical stranger. She
practices her kicks with the heels on and finds
she has worked her middle so much that she can
maintain balance. She's a pretty, dancing clown.
She smiles at herself and one of the youngest girls
comes up to her and links arms and they practice

together – saying *dah dah dah* – and falling into laughter at their exaggerated selves. Joan wiggles her hips and eyebrows together. The younger girl guffaws. The costume has let something loose inside Joan. On the stage, she will be alight like the desert in the nuclear blast, and just as uncaring.

HE BROKE HER HEART often. He would be a stranger to her, often, and that's what breaks the heart. When she miscarried the second time, it was hard to tell him through all the tears. She'd gone to the hospital alone. She missed her mother. Faith had tried to be her friend, she knew, but she couldn't seem to let her. Her heart had room for one large person. She watched the midday movies. Bette Davis was her friend. Katherine Hepburn and Lauren Bacall. The words came out of her mouth, 'I've lost the baby.' And for a moment his eyes showed relief. She saw it before he could hide it, before his brow furrowed and he pulled her to him and he kissed the top of her head. A wave of rage flowed through her, and revulsion. He was relieved. She saw it. Nothing could take that away. He was a stranger. He didn't want to be her family. He didn't want a family. He never would.

THE YOUNG DANCER IS called Angel and she asks Joan for a cocktail after rehearsal. Joan fights an apprehension that is the old her and they sit in a corner booth in the The Mint and Angel has something with pineapple in it while Joan has her martini with a twist. They are ravenous from the exercise, so they order hot dogs in soft buns, and laugh at the sauces dripping down their fingers. To Joan's surprise Angel does not talk a lot, but seems happy to sit and drink and smoke and watch people coming in and out of the bar. Joan feels comfortable to tell her she appreciates this.

'It's nice to have some relaxed company,' she says.

'It is,' says Angel. 'Small talk is for small minds.'

Joan grins at her – the sides of her face are rusty, like the Tin Man's joints. The smile is genuine. What if she had just been in the wrong place for eighteen years? Had been the whole wrong person?

'Oh, here's my one o'clock,' says Angel. She points to a slim, silver-haired man in a suit, who has just walked in the bar. 'He's not big on small talk either.' She winks. He sees her and begins to walk over. Angel stands and gives Joan an earnest look: 'You okay to get home, honey?'

'Sure.' Joan nods, does not show shock – Joan would not be shocked. Angel leans down and gives her a gentle kiss on the cheek. 'See you soon.'

'You will.'

She watches them walk away – the dark suit and the mauve shimmer. She is concerned for Angel, despite herself. Is it different than giving them cocktails and coins, than dancing for them, to be paid for that? Or is it better than giving it away for free, for comfort? Why did Angel see Joan as an ally? Were the other girls in better circumstances and therefore judged her? Was it purely Joan's age – did that make her seem more likely to have seen it all, to accept?

That night she did not go to Oliver, or to Harvey. She lay alone with her hands over her abdomen, TV blaring.

THE BABY SCREAMED AND he frowned and turned up the TV. She took the baby into the bedroom.

The noise crowded her. Her heart raced sickly. Twenty-seven children killed in a bus accident in Prestonburg, Kentucky, said the news, while her child gasped for air.

There were two bugs smeared across the blind, she saw. The blind had been rolled up and down and the bugs had been trapped and they'd been squashed and smeared.

She lay down with the squealing baby and kissed his tiny red forehead and he didn't stop and she hovered her hand across his mouth and then took it away and kissed him again, as sweetly as she could.

SHE SHOWS UP AT Oliver's and a short, thick-haired man answers the door.

'Yes?'

'Oh, I was just coming to see Oliver.'

'Ollie is busy,' he says.

She peeks in and sees a pack of men in dark suits through a haze of cigar smoke. Oliver looks at her, then the man at the door, and gives the man a signal: *make her go away.*

She sees cards on the table, bottles of liquor, and then, two scantily clad women bringing in trays. Both blonde, young. One of them – Angel.

The man raises his eyebrow at her. 'You gotta go, sweetheart.'

'Alright,' Joan says, trying not to show confusion. Joan would cope with anything, would know about these things, the ways of men like this, the tasks of Angels. The door closes in her face. Had Oliver gotten Angel into the show, too? Is that why she sought Joan out, because she saw her arrive with him?

The next day, Oliver calls her at the motel. 'I told you to always call ahead.'

'I'm sorry,' she says.

'It's all just business.' His voice is gentle and matter of fact.

'I think I understand.'

'You do?' He sounds relieved.

'Men mix business with pleasure.'

'That's right, honey.'

Joan twirls the phone cord around her finger. She's not exactly sure what Joan would do. She thinks of telling him she never wants to see him again. She has been too understanding. But then, he is not trying to cover up what he is – there is not really a defence in the explanation. But can she trust her own judgement? Never. Never again. She can only go with what's offered, not think. There really is no worry left. She worried to completion.

She still has nothing to say.

'Joan, will you let me put you in a nicer place than that motel?'

'Will I let you?'

'Alright, I will set it up.'

'Alright. But I want to be the only one with a key. It'll be my own. And you have to call ahead, too.'

'You are a classy broad, Joan. I'm not sure I deserve you.'

'I'm not sure anyone deserves what they end up getting.'

She hears him inhaling smoke, sighing it out.
'I'll call you with the details later.'
He hangs up.

THEIR CHILD WAS TWO years old and her mother couldn't stand not having met him. She used all of the family savings to come over. She would stay for a month or more.

In the lead-up, Jack spent more time in the room with the closed door. He played the same chords over and over again.

In the lead-up, her chest became tighter. Food tasted slimy and off. She only wanted white bread, a little butter. Cups of tea. Sometimes she found she had been staring at the bright window in the dark lounge room until it was just a square on her eye. The child stared at his mother staring. At toddler-age, he was good and quiet. He knew he could lie for a long time in mother's flesh; he knew he could get a little pat on the head from dad, but that dad would go away into the room if he talked too much. He liked his little wooden train and it was best he played with it on the carpet, to muffle the sound of the wheels.

Her mother arrived and took some rest and Jack was his show-off self, very accommodating, and she thought, with tense curiosity, it would be interesting to see how long he could keep this up.

As much as possible, she took her mother and her child out of the cardboard house. They wandered the large furniture and appliance stores; they sat in a diner; they went for drives, and her mother made comments about America, about how big and friendly and shiny it all was.

She was glad her mother was having a good time. She was glad America could put on a show for her mother.

One night, they were all watching television, about two weeks into the stay. Jack had managed to still be performative, and seemed to genuinely want to accommodate her mother, though in bed at night he fell straight to sleep, as though worn out, and was not tender with her. It was as though he was punishing her for bringing someone into the house to whom he must divert his attention. She was sorry. She knew he only had so much to give.

They were watching television, a crime show about real killers, and it was sensationalised and frightening. Jack did not make a move to change it to accommodate her mother. But her mother seemed just as drawn into it, though she made little sounds of shock.

'I used to think,' said her mother in a break, 'that we were all capable of such horror – that all it would take is a moment, something to snap us out of ourselves. But having lived long enough now, I see that most of these killers have something in common.'

A neat, smiling woman on the TV sold washing powder.

She didn't want her mother to go on. The hairs were raised on her neck because she could feel him, his thoughts.

'All these men have been broken by their mothers and fathers, by their school days, or by women. And sometimes a succession of these beatings means that one day, they just tip over.'

She could not hear for the blood in her ears.

'Maybe,' Jack replied, but she could see he had moved outside of himself – the way he stared ahead and the way his features had gone stiff. She wondered if her mother was attuned to the way he could snap out of himself. It had taken her a while to notice, longer to understand it would keep happening, and longer to know how to be around it. How to take the fear into her own body, sharing the burden. It was much, much harder with someone else here, and it had also been harder since the baby had been born. She was more likely to avoid than engage, now. To distance herself. And receive a physical shock, a jolt of electricity, then, when his hand grazed hers, when he pulled her in for a hug or decided to fuck her, and most of all, when his eyes met hers.

With her mother here she had to find ways of being herself. And she had forgotten how to do that. So there were long silences, which she and her mother never used to have. And so they visited the furniture and appliance stores and places where they could look at things and comment on them, for something to talk about.

That night in bed his eyes were open. He was sweating as though having a nightmare. She clicked on the small TV in their bedroom, put it on a low murmur. She gave him space but touched a toe to his shin under the blankets. Cold sparks travelled up and down her spine. She wanted her mother to go home.

THE SUITE IS BROWNS and greens, a tropical jungle aesthetic. Large windows and desert view. Plenty of room to walk around. Joan has the only key, or so he says. And she has already brought Harvey here, because she can mix business and pleasure, too, because she likes him and because she wants to have secrets, the way men do.

She has also given Angel the address and one night she knocks on the door at two a.m. and Joan puts on a robe and lets her in. She sits in a lounge chair and Joan makes her a cup of coffee instead of the bourbon she has asked for. Angel says she is sore and tired. Joan cannot be any kind of hero, but she says Angel can stay there. She doesn't know if she will regret it because it has been easier to be alone – to have the air around her after those eighteen years; the air and space like the wide, bright desert, like the wind of the blast.

She lets Angel sleep on the other side of the King bed and it feels okay, just a gentle, young presence. After a few nights she does, in fact, prefer Angel comes back here. She makes her a coffee and they go to sleep. They don't talk a lot but it's a different not-talking – it is without tension. They wake up late and read with the sun streaming in, in their separate favourite spots in the big suite. Angel reads romance novels. Joan reads memoirs about grisly childhoods, alcoholism, and books about serial murderers.

One day she asks Angel about her parents.

'They live in Mississippi,' she says. 'They think I'm a hairdresser.' She smiles. 'I do miss them, but I was always different.'

Joan finishes her letter to home that day. It is a complete fabrication, a performance. She writes 'we' this, and 'we' that. 'We' are on holiday in Vegas – finally, a holiday, away from the cardboard house! She cannot write her child's name.

IT IS A FULL house for the show but Joan cannot really see the crowd. When she comes out at the top of the stairs, smiling and sashaying, there is just hot light and music. Her upper lip sweats under the thick powder. Her trained muscles lift and curve and stretch. This moment where, one by one, the dancers turn and tip up one hip and look back coyly – a line of promise. This part where the leg arcs up and around has always tugged at something in her abdomen, and right now, in the third number, tears rush to her eyes as she does this – up and around, back up and around. Why does it unleash this now? *Stay right here*, she says to herself. *This is all you need to be: warmly lit.* If they could even turn it up a little. Because her insides have turned cold.

Backstage between numbers her water glass slips from her trembling fingers. 'Just adrenaline,' Angel says, and her voice sounds far away. 'Channel it. You're doing great.' The outfits on the hanger shimmer like snakes. There are black circles around each of the lights on the dresser mirror and they spot her eyes. Her mouth tastes like ash.

They are rushed back out.

He had not looked dead.

No. Joan must dance. Just dance. *Not now.*

He had looked like a sleeping child, curled up next to his father, who was in a more twisted shape, and covered in vomit – his mouth arched back and his hands in fists. All Jack had wanted was peace, once, now, forever.

Joan's knees collapse beneath her, when the line moves past the front of the stage. She takes two girls down with her. She is shaking so violently her teeth are smashing up against each other.

Jack mustn't have trusted that she could make it right for the boy. Or else why would he have taken him from her?

A man and a boy. And all the years she gave him – dead too.

She is lying on a couch backstage, her arms locked, her face locked, making no noise, but she can feel the hot spill of tears and snot. There is too much light, now. It is everywhere. She is hollow. The light will crisp her shell and turn it to dust.

JOAN DOES NOT STAY in bed for days. That is not what Joan would do. Joan tells Angel to mix her a martini and she sits up and her head spins but she takes a few sips, as though it were medicine, and she gets up and partially opens the blinds. She sits back down and sighs.

It was not a breakdown. Just something delayed, and uncontainable.

'I'm going to order you some food,' Angel says. 'What do you most feel like?'

'Chicken,' Joan says.

Angel dials for food and then sits in her favourite chair and opens her novel. She is not going to ask, Joan realises. Out of politeness or diffidence?

The chicken and slaw arrives and they tear at strips of it with their fingers.

'You have a car, don't you?' Angel says.

'I do.'

'I've been saving money,' Angel says. 'No one knows. Oliver doesn't know.'

'What would you like to do?'

'Maybe go to LA, maybe go to college – learn something useful, but still dance, you know?'

It is sunny in LA, too, Joan thinks. Maybe she

could work in a shop, help other women find their costumes, their various selves.

She can only keep going with what's offered, not think.

'It's meant to be healthy and relaxed there, too. Could be good if more of your past comes up like that.'

'How do you know it was that?'

'You call out his name. You have nightmares.'

'Jack?'

'No, Sammy.'

'Oh.' Joan cannot stomach any more of the food.

'Maybe you can tell me what happened one day,' Angel says gently.

'I don't need to.' It feels wrong to be looked after, especially by a woman so much younger than her.

Angel stands up and goes around behind Joan and puts her hands in Joan's hair, massaging. A powerful satisfaction comes over Joan's body. 'My mum used to do this for me,' Angel says.

Joan sighs.

'I have to write a letter to my mother, to tell her what happened,' Joan says. 'I haven't been able to. Finding the words...'

'I'm sure there is time.'

Joan's brow unknots, and she slowly gives in to the soothing touch, closes her eyes. She will never talk about Jack – she will leave him behind the locked door of that room, playing those chords, over and over. But perhaps she will tell Angel about Sammy. And one day she will go home to see her mother. But not until she feels has been somewhat replenished, after the blast.

ANGELA MEYER'S DEBUT NOVEL, *A Superior Spectre*, has been shortlisted for an Australian Book Industry Award, the MUD Literary Prize and an Aurealis Award. Her writing has been widely published, including in *Best Australian Stories, Island, The Big Issue, The Australian, The Lifted Brow* and *Killings.* She has also published a book of flash fiction, *Captives.* She has worked in bookstores, as a book reviewer, in a whisky bar, and for the past few years has published a range of Australian authors for Echo Publishing, including award-winners and an international number one bestseller. She grew up in Northern New South Wales and lives in Melbourne, Australia.

A Superior Spectre

JEFF IS DYING. HAUNTED by memories, grappling with shame, he runs away from his home in Melbourne to rural Scotland with a piece of beta tech that allows him to enter the mind of someone in the past. Instructed to use it no more than three times, Jeff – self-indulgent, isolated and deteriorating – is in no mood to play by the rules.

In the 1860s, Leonora lives in the Highlands, surrounded by nature. Her contented life and a secret romantic friendship with the local laird are interrupted when her father sends her to live with her aunt in Edinburgh. But Leonora's ability to embrace her new life is shadowed by a dark presence that begins to lurk behind her eyes, and strange visions that threaten her sanity.

A novel about curiosity, entitlement and manipulation, about voyeurism, control and self-doubt, this imaginative, bold debut asks provocative questions about identity and the boundaries of the self.

"Brilliant ... unapologetically feminist rage, passion and awareness." BOOKS+PUBLISHING

"Lyrical, literary and visceral." SYDNEY MORNING HERALD